MR. MALIN AND THE NIGHT

WILLIAM PAULEY III

CB555-03: Mr. Malin and the Night
ISBN: 978-0-9962768-6-3
Library of Congress Control Number: 2016931722

Carrion Blue 555
Chicopee MA / Lambertville NJ
carrionblue555@gmail.com

Front cover art copyright ©2016 by Zack Rezendes.
Cover design ©2016 by Matthew Revert.
www.matthewrevert.com
Carrion Blue 555 logo designed by Brent Carpentier.

Mr. Malin and the Night originally appeared in *LIVINHELL*.
This reissued edition ©2016 by William Pauley III.
Interior illustrations ©2016 by Zack Rezendes.
Additional content copyright ©2016 by its respective author(s).

"This is Heaven alright, but there's a man outside with a gun."
—Cardiacs, "What Paradise is Like"

TABLE OF CONTENTS

AN EXORCISM OF WILLIEZ
An Introduction by Joseph Bouthiette Jr.
v

MR. MALIN AND THE NIGHT
SIR William Pauley III
9

GABBY vs. WILLIEZ
An Interview with Gabino Iglesias
cxxxiii

GETTING FUCKED
An Afterword by Stephanie M. Wytovich
clv

AN EXORCISM OF WILLIEZ
An Introduction by Josh Myers
by Joseph Bouthiette Jr.

Hi, I'm Josh Myers.

You may know me as the author of such indie published flops as *Feast of Oblivion*, *GUNS*, or *Haiku Fuck You* (released simultaneously with this volume), though likely not.

You are more likely to know me as the guy who'd get blackout drunk and text William Pauley III provocative messages and demand we "get hitched."

What a mistake that was.

Because I'm Josh Myers, it took me longer to learn what most people currently understand as common knowledge: William Pauley III is a fucking psychopath.

He must be stopped.

We need to obtain the seven sacred daggers and *take him down.*

He is, quite literally, the Devil.

Hey, this book is about the Devil.

Shit, spoiler alert.

NO. NO I LIED. THIS BOOK IS CERTAINLY NOT ABOUT THE DEVIL. I AM VERY GOOD AT MAKING SOMETHING SOUND LIKE A SPOILER WHEN IT'S REALLY NOT, LIKE WHEN JOE READ SPOILERS FOR THE NEW *STAR WARS* MOVIE AND I WANTED TO TRY TO MAKE HIM BELIEVE THAT THOSE WEREN'T ACTUALLY SPOILERS BUT THEN HE

SAW THE MOVIE AND REALIZED THAT THOSE WERE SPOILERS ANYWAYS. NO DEVIL HERE. I HAVE NOT BEEN DRINKING. FUCK YOU NO I HAVEN'T.

William Pauley III is the Devil, but in that charming, ridiculously handsome, socially and sexually attractive to everyone he meets sort of way.

He's the man that can set his friend on fire in one instant and be getting free lap dances at the strip bar the next.

Worse yet, he's procreated, and his influence will irreversibly affect the innocent boy that could have been, *should have been*, gifted to any other loving family.

Most recently he's gone so far as to corrupt fellow author Stephanie M. Wytovich, my best friend (I am Josh), into being general supreme of his hellspawn army.

The glee he gets from it all is nauseating—his happiness disgusts me.

Be warned, reader.

This man is not to be trusted, his smile not to be followed.

He will break your heart, as he has mine.

Josh.

That's me.

I'm Josh.

Joseph Bouthiette Jr.
Spring 2016

The author would like to thank the good folks at Carrion Blue 555 for publishing this special ten year anniversary edition of Mr. Malin and the Night, *especially Joseph Bouthiette Jr. and Josh Myers.*

Also, thank you to all the contributors: Stephanie M. Wytovich, Gabino Iglesias, Matthew Revert, and Zack Rezendes. Thank you for making this book so special!

And last, but certainly not least, thank you to everyone who supported my work in my first ten years of writing. Your support means everything to me. If you are one of the very few people who actually own one of the original printed copies of this book, show it to me and you will receive free hugs for life.

Hi, I'm Williez.

See you in ten more years!

MR. MALIN

AND THE

NIGHT

*What would you do if the Devil
gave you one more night to live?*

"All things move toward their end."
—Nick Cave

I thought long and hard about the course of events that went down tonight.
I thought long.
I thought hard.
She's dead.
Evey's dead and I'm dead with her.
Our bodies lay strewn against wet concrete.
But the plan was foolproof!
The plan was perfect!
The plan was wrong...
The plan was flawed...
> *we were fucked in every way.*
>> *fucked in every goddamned fucking way.*
Dead at 29.
Fucking 29!
I had plans for the rest of my life!
I had things to do!
Things that needed to be done!
And now I'm dead.
DEAD!
Dead at fucking 29 years old.

And Evey.
Poor beautiful Evey...
                              only 24.
Dead at 24.

She was so beautiful.
A Picasso.
A real fucking piece of art.
And she lies beside me now.
Her beauty wasted.
Dead.
Both of us.
Dead.

Our souls and our bones are all that remain.

Do you love me?
Do you love me?
Do you love me?
Evey's words echo throughout every wrinkle in my
brain.

Well, do you?
Vincent?

Valentine's Day.
We're sitting here at The Alexis,
the nicest restaurant in town,
when she comes out with it.
What a bunch of bullshit.
Does she even love me?
It feels like she's just using this holiday as an
excuse to *feel love.*
And to *be loved.*

Shit.
I know.

I *know* she fucking loves me.
And I love her.
I know I love her.
Fuck.
Fuck.
Fuck.
I can't love her.
But what can a man say to those big blue eyes?

YOU FUCKING ASSHOLE!

Evey slams her wine glass against the table,
cutting her hand on the broken shards,
and storms out of the restaurant.
I don't move.
Somehow I knew the night would end like this.
Everyone around me sits, staring.
I calmly pull out my wallet, lay a couple hundreds
on the table and leave.
Evey is standing by the car.
She must have forgotten I drove tonight.
We get in the car and don't speak a word for the
first ten minutes.
All I wanted was to go home.
I look over at Evey.
She has the cloth napkin from the restaurant
wrapped around her bloody hand.

Are you okay?
Fuck you.
No, fuck you, Evey. You did this to yourself.
GODDAMMIT! I'M FINE!

Silence.
Evey, on the verge of tears, speaks...

> *Why don't you love me, Vincent?*

She says these words under her breath, while looking out the passenger-side window.

> Evey...

I barely get out her name before she interrupts.

> *It's her, isn't it?*
> *You still love her, don't you?*
> Evey...

She interrupts again.

> *Vincent, she left you!*
> *She isn't coming back.*
> GODDAMMIT, EVEY!

I shout.
It's quiet the rest of the way home.

For the last three months or so,
Evey and I have been living together.
I know.
She's right.
I *am* an asshole.
But maybe she would understand if only she knew the truth.

If I didn't have to hide from her.
Only then could my reasoning be justified.
But she'd still be gone.
I know that.
Goddammit, how did I get to be so fucking stupid?
Why *her*?
Why *Evey*?
Fuck.
I *can't* love her.

I pull into the driveway.
Evey and I get out and walk to the door.
I look into her eyes, but only for a second.
I want to tell her.
I want to tell her I love her.
I want to tell her I love her and her only.
I turn away and unlock the door.

Evey walks straight to the bathroom to clean
herself up.
Her makeup is a running mess from crying.
Why do I treat this girl the way I do?
I go and lie down on our bed, feet to the floor.
I close my eyes.
I used to be able to close my eyes and see only
black,
but all I see now is her face.
Amy.
God, I *do* miss her.
But it's *Evey* that I love.
I only wish she knew that.
Jesus Christ, why do I treat this girl the way I do?

Evey leaves the bathroom and leans herself against
the frame of the bedroom doorway.
She's calmed down.
She looks sweet, but cautious still.
I can tell by the way she's breathing that the
argument is over.

> *Vincent, I'm sorry.*
> *I didn't mean...*
> Baby, come here.

As much as I know I love her, I still don't want
Evey around all that much.
She can really fuck things up for me.
Mentally.
Emotionally.
As much as I know I love her, I still tell myself *no*.
I still turn myself off to her.
I still stand by this brick wall I've built around
myself.
You can't come in, Evey.
I'm sorry.
I want you more than anything.
More than the world.
I'm sorry.
You can't come in.
The pictures (*when they smile*) make it all seem
worthwhile.
But words are just as long as they are thin.
You can't come in.
Even as I lie beside her now, I still feel distant.
I still feel cold.

MR. MALIN AND THE NIGHT

I still feel empty.
She has everything needed to make me into an honest man.
Everything needed to make me right.
Everything needed to make me.
I have everything needed to shut her down.
Everything needed to put her out.
Everything needed to fuck up all she has going for her.
I can't do it.
Why am I here?
I know what I need to do.
Why the fuck am I here?
I need to be gone.
I need to be gone.
I need to be gone.
Why am I still lying beside her?
Fuck.
I love her.
With all my heart I love her.
I'm afraid.
I'm afraid she'll find out the truth.
I'm afraid I will hurt her.
I'm afraid to love her.
I'm afraid.

Evey smiles. I smile. She seems to think I know her. And her, me.
She *seems...*
She moves around me, from one side of the bed to the other.
She stands.

She's beautiful.
She often looks down to stare at her dress.
Her dress.
It hugs her every curve.
She's beautiful.
She sings and holds out her hand to touch mine.
My heart s
          i
          n
          k
          s.

Was there ever a better time?
Vincent, your heart is as big as mine.
You're lost. I'm lost.
But in the end, will it even matter?

In the end...
She's breaking down the brick wall.
I'm watching her as she swings.
Every word delivers a shattering blow.
She's breaking it.
She doesn't even know.
She's breaking it down with every word she
speaks.
She's breaking it.

My dear Evey.
I have a choice to make.
To stay here with you,
or to leave and never look back.
The one thing I *must* do is the only thing I *can't*

do.
If I leave now, I will *always* look back.
I will *always* see that dress.
I will *always* see that smile.
I will remember your voice and
your words will haunt me.
It's true.
I've already fucked up.
I pull her back into bed.
I wrap my arms around her.

I love you.
I love you, too.

She is in.
The bricks are now dust at my feet.
More than ever, *she is in*.

I've always been told if you lead a good life, you
will be rewarded with eternal life.
Golden streets.
Rivers of wine.
Wings.
Harps.
Angels singing.
Pearly gates.
There's never a rainy day in Heaven.
The problem with this is that I've always
enjoyed the rain.
Always.
Maybe it's the easiest explanation for all that I've
done.
Maybe the fact that I love the rain
led me to be the way I am now.
Or was...
   I still can't believe I'm fucking dead.

Well, either way, it doesn't really matter.
The fact is, I *didn't* lead a good life.

I'll never see those golden streets.
I'll never drink from any river of wine.
I'll never even see those fucking pearly gates
unless I'm standing on the outside
looking in.

Honestly, I still feel alive.
I still think.
I still have memories.
But I can't see for shit.
I'm in total darkness.
I can't feel my body.
I can't move my arms.
I can't feel the bullet wound in my forehead.
There is absolutely no pain.
I can't even feel the ground I'm lying on.
It's a strange fucking feeling.

*I can't help but think that something should be
happening.*
To me.
My spirit.
Whatever the fuck I am now.
Is this it?
Is this all there is?
Is this even existence?

> *Why the fuck are you just lying there?*

A voice calls to me.
I say nothing.
I mean, I'm dead.

I must be...

> *You've been down there for*
> *forty-five fucking minutes.*
> *Get the fuck up.*

Still I say nothing.

> *Man, get the fuck up!*

A fist stuffs into my chest.
When I say "*my chest*" I mean "*my body.*"
And when I say "*my body*" I mean "*this fucking corpse I've been lying in.*"
He roughly pulls me [a ghost?] to my feet.
He either doesn't realize his strength or is just put out with me.
Either way, I want to be gone.
I want to be anywhere but here.
My sight returns now in full focus.
I can see the body of the voice.
He is a black man about six feet tall. He wears dark sunglasses,
even though it's nighttime.
He has long, confusing sideburns that nearly touch his goatee and hair so messy it reminds me of smoke and flame.
It looks as if he hasn't washed it in weeks.
Colors jet black with a touch of gray evenly spread throughout.
He has a slight gap between his upper front middle teeth, but you can only see it when he

smiles.
And he never smiles.
He wears a lot of jewelry.
Rings.
Bracelets.
Necklaces.
All of them made of silver.
He looks like a fucking pimp from Hell.
His clothing is all black.
T-shirt.
Leather pants.
Boots.
Leather trench coat.
His belt is black and held together with a silver ankh at the buckle.
He carries a consistent look of anger.
It's hard to tell exactly what he's thinking.
I study my new design.
I seem to be in the same form.
Same face.
Same body.
Same clothes, even.
I touch my forehead.
The same fucking bullet wound.
I look exactly like the body at my feet.
The body I managed to fuck up in just 29 years.

> *You're dead.*
> Yeah, I've noticed.

I point to the bullet hole in my forehead.

How long have you been standing there?
Long enough to see the end.
Did you see her die?

He lowers his sunglasses.

Who?
Evey. Did you see h—

I look back for her, but there is only my body.
A lump forms in my throat.
Could she still be alive?
Did she survive?
What.
The.
Fuck.
Is.
Going.
On?

B E N !

She's alive?

I think hard about my sweet Evey.
I have to figure this out.
We were both shot!
I saw the bullet go through her chest!
I saw her die!

WHAT THE FUCK IS GOING ON?

MR. MALIN AND THE NIGHT

Ben fucked me over.

That's what the fuck is going on!

B e n , t h a t m o t h e r f u c k e r !
H e f u c k e d m e o v e r !

I turn around and walk over to where her body
once lay.
There are no sounds to my footsteps.
I notice this immediately.
There is no blood on the pavement.

He fucked me over!
But I saw her die!

The man patiently lets me gather my thoughts.
He pulls out a package of hand-rolled cigarettes.
He slides one out and pushes it to his lips.
With a flip, a strike, and a flame, he breathes
smoke.
I can feel the nicotine flowing through my veins.
It's not there, of course,
but 15 years of smoking really fucks with you.
You can't even look at a person smoking without
feeling the need to smoke.
Your body starts reacting as if the person in front
of you is *you*.
That is now *your* cigarette.
Those are now *your* lips.
That is now *your* nicotine pulsing through *your*
veins.

And I need it.
I've had a rough day…
      to say the very fucking least.

                        So who the fuck are you?
                        You can call me Gonn.
                        Gonn?
                        Gonn.

I point to my chest.

                        Vincent.
            Oh, I already know your name, Mr. Malin.

He takes another long draw from his cigarette.

                        How the fuck do you know my name?
                        Who the fuck are you?
                        I told you. I am Gonn.
                        I've come for your soul, Mr. Malin.

My heart sinks.
It can't be over now.
I have too many questions that need to be answered.
I have to find Evey.
I have to figure out what the fuck happened.
I have too many questions that need to be answered.
It can't be over now.
It can't.

> Look, Gonn...
> *You want to know where the girl is?*

I pause.
Evey, where are you?
Are you with Ben?
Hot blood pulses through my veins.
That fucking bastard!
What the fuck is he doing with her?
If Ben so much as touches a hair on her head...
FUCK!

> That's only *one* of *many* questions I have at this
> point.

I say this as calmly as I can, trying not to let my
anger show through.
But it does.

> *Well, you're in luck my friend.*
> *I've come here to make a deal with you.*
> *I'm willing to give you the time to take care of*
> business,
> *no questions asked,*
> *as long as you can do three things for me.*
> What things?
> *The rules, Mr. Malin. The terms of departure.*

I want to leave.
I want to find Evey.
I hear him out.

Before I let you go, you must know the rules.
Failure to cooperate will result in your night
falling short and a fast trip to Hell.

I can feel him staring me down, even through those dark fucking shades.

Number one: *If you feel the need to end a life,*
don't.
Make he or she do it themselves.

I try to interrupt. He holds up two fingers, cigarette resting between them, not missing a beat.

Number two: *You will be given a donor body.*
YES, the living will be able to see you.
NO, your body is not invincible.
Anything that happens while you are in this body,
you will feel, taste, and ache.
YES, your body can die, and if it does you will
cross over.
Number three: *You have until dawn.*
Any questions?

So many...
He looks pissed.
I only ask one.

Can I bum a smoke?
Fuck off, kid, you're dead.

He still has that pissed off, stern fucking look on

his face.
Fuck him.

So do we have a deal?
Are you fucking serious?
Yeah. Hell yeah. I'll do whatever you want.
Are you fucking with me?
I mean, who the fuck are you... the Devil or
something?

Gonn takes a final draw from his cigarette, flicks it
off to the side and walks toward me.
He exhales.

Let's get started.

I turn around and follow him back down the alley I
last walked just an hour before.
Then alive.
Now dead.

The sun seeps in through the blinds of the window.
Rays of pure white sunlight burn out my eyes as I sleep.
I awaken.
Evey is still at my side, still asleep, still dreaming.
I don't want to wake her.
I slide out from beneath her arm and stand on the floor beside her.
I look down at her.
She fell asleep in her dress.
Her perfect blue dress that fits her body so snug.

I walk to the bathroom and wash my face in the sink.
The water brings me into full consciousness.
With two handfuls of water I instantly become more aware.
More awake.
I reach for a towel and dry my face.
My face.

It's been so long since I've *really* taken a look at myself.
I look in the mirror.
I look tired.
My eyes scream black at the daylight.
I need to shave.
My hair is starting to get long and seems to grow darker as the days go by.
I have ghostly pale skin.
Maybe that's what's making my hair seem darker, my skin.
I need to sleep.
I can't sleep.
But I need to sleep.
I stare down each and every feature.
I stare for nearly twenty minutes.

I decide to take a shower.
This is what I need now, I convince myself.
I need to think.
I need to relax.
I need to feel the hot water race down my skin.
I need to think.
I need to relax.
I bend down and turn the knobs.
Water rushes out of the faucet.
I run my hand through the flow.
It needs to be hotter.
I adjust the knobs.
Perfect.
I pull up on the lever.
Two seconds later the water from the faucet now

comes from the showerhead above.
I take off my clothes and step in.
The water gives me exactly what I need.
I need to think.
I need to relax.
I close my eyes.
I breathe.
In and out.
In and out.
I breathe.
I'm a mess.
A complete wreck.
I breathe.
What the fuck am I doing here?
Evey.
Why Evey?
We've only known each other for three months.
She could still be anybody.
She could still be holding back.
I don't *really* know her.
I have an *idea.*
But an *idea* is not enough.
I love her.
But I don't *know* her.
I love her.
But *love* is not enough.
An *idea* is not enough and *love* is not enough.
I don't *know* her.
She could be anybody.
I love her.
But *love* is not enough.
I breathe.

In and out.
In and out.
I breathe.
I stand and let the hot water pour down my body.
I need to think.
I need to relax.

I see a shadow appear from the corner of my eye.
A figure is moving on the other side of the shower curtain.
The shadow gets clearer.
The shadow gets darker.
A hand.
A hand slowly pulls back the curtain.
Evey.
She peeks in.

Mind if I join?

I motion for her to come in.
She smiles and takes off her clothes.
That dress.
That perfect blue dress now rests at her feet.
It's now I see that it wasn't the dress that was perfect, it was her.
Every inch.
Every strand.
Every curve.
Her right leg steps into the shower and quickly retracts.

Wow, that's really hot!

I let out a short laugh.

Oh, sorry about that.

I adjust the knobs.
The water cools down in seconds.

Okay, it's safe now.

I smile.
She laughs.
Her leg returns, this time followed by the rest of her.
She stands in front of me.
My eyes follow up her leg, through a long and distracted journey to her eyes.
Her body is beautiful.
Perfect in *every way*.
Her eyes catch mine wandering.
She smiles.
We both smile.
She extends her arms out in front of her and weaves them between my arms and my body, and she pulls me closer.
Our bodies now touching.
She is beautiful.
I can't help myself when she looks at me.
When I see those eyes.
Those beautiful blue eyes.
When she stares into mine.
She is beautiful.
I kiss her.

Soft, her white skin.
Hands slither, arms wrap, lips cover.
I keep her little hands in mine.
I love her.
The more she's around me, the more I know it's true.
I love her.
Tongues swirl, lips curl, teeth to lips.
She wraps her right leg around me.
She pulls my hips hard against hers.
Her lips crashing into mine like a violent sea.
Her tongue wants.
Her lips need.
Her hips, hungry.
I push myself inside of her.
We're both in ecstasy.
I love her.
I know I love her.
I'm *afraid* to love her.
But I do.

I do.

...love *is* enough.

It takes us a good half hour,
but finally we get to the donor's house.
Just by the looks of the place,
I can tell Gonn is giving me a *user*.
The yard is unkempt and standing nearly waist
high
and the entire left-hand side of the porch is caved
in.
As we walk inside, I notice the wallpaper is stained
a deep yellow and in many parts is curling over,
exposing the chipping pale blue paint underneath.
I've come across some pretty shady-looking people
in my life, but nothing compares to the shit-trap
body Gonn is showing me now.

This is it.
This is what?
Your new home for the next 6 hours.
Get in. Try it out.
Are you fucking kidding me?
This asshole is so fucked up,

I may as well take MY fucking body out there!
I mean, the only reason I even need another body
is because
I need to be able to be seen without raising
suspicion, right?
R i g h t...
THIS IS *THE* MOST SUSPICIOUS-LOOKING
FUCK OUT THERE!
*Look, if there was another recently deceased in
the radius of 30 miles
then you could have HIM, but this is it.
He's all we have.*
Fuck.

I pause. Calm down. Concede.

How did he die?

I ask as if I don't already know.

*Heroin.
Which brings us to your next concern.*
What?
This guy's blood is still thick with it.

I put my hands over my face and try my
damnedest not to scream.

How the fuck am I supposed to do this, Gonn?

He smiles.

>   *That's your problem. Now get in.*
>   *Time is wasting.*

As much as I'd like to rip his fucking head off, he's
right.
Time is wasting.
Six hours and counting.
After that, time will never be an issue again.
This will be the last six hours I walk this earth.
No time to waste.
I step inside the junkie's limp body.
ImM e ***D*** ia t eLy
I   fe E l
T he   e F F *ec* T s.
I   s tUm **blE**   a LL   ovEr   thE
fUckIng
    p L   a cE.
I ' M   soo oO   Fu ckE d   u**P.**

>   *How do you feel?*

G O   nn—*smI*Li ng.
I tR*y* t O   sPEak—

>   F-F-Fuck... Y...ou.

Bbb   bl o   Oo**d**   riv   E eers   run
ccOldD.
I   ttt R*y* tOo   sT *anD.*
I cc aAn   F*fe*EEel   tHe   dDrr Ug g
ssLug gggGggi s sH h l   p ulli Ng   aAt   *mM* y
F   *eeet,*

bUt nO ThiN g **cOme**S mOore thA n a
  tWi t cH.
T*h*He *r*ooOm   sPi ns aRou Nd mE.
*CooL*ors *aNd* dark Ness.
Col**Or**s aNd Dar*kn*Ess.
                I ssEe
              It ***aLL***.
I sE *E* Sh AdO   wS   dA nCin G
  aRounD tHe ro oM.
theY siN g an***D*** they tAu nt mE!
T hEy dAre mE tO   mOve!
T*Hey*   lAugH   aNd   **tHe**y crA*w*L
  baCk
iNto *thee*   daRk.
VoicEs   sp iN nin G.
C**o**Lo rs sHiftiNg.
GoNn griNn iNg.

I *vo* miT.

FaDe.

How many times have I sat here searching for the right thing to say?
The right thing to do?
Who the hell am I?
Who is Vincent Malin?
These are the questions I am constantly asking myself.
Really it doesn't even matter,
I know the answers aren't coming tonight.
There is nothing I can think about that I haven't already thought a million times before.
My mind is a flooded sea of unanswered questions.
I'm drowning.
I'm sick of searching.
I'm tired of trying.
Fed up with mistakes.

Some say it's what you do that defines you.
I'm a mechanic,
and in a way it really does define me.

I understand how things work,
I can build something from nothing,
and I'm not afraid to get my hands dirty.
But what is it that drives me?
What is it that gives me a reason to live?

I have no children.
I was married... *once.*
All of my friends are mere acquaintances.

At times I wonder who would attend my funeral.
If I were to die at this moment,
would anyone mourn me?
Whose tears will fall when they hear the news?
Of all the faces I've known,
Evey's is the only one I can see.
Every other face is a clouded blur with muted
screams.
They are the ghosts that haunt me.
Evey is the only one who seems to genuinely care.

There's my answer.

It's Evey.
She's the glass of worth that gives
meaning to my long days.
Her body aches for mine the same way I do for
hers.
I wasn't so sure before, but I am certain of it now.
It's a strange stronghold, this love.
Her voice.
I can feel it.

I can keep it.
It is mine.
Her lips may be the death of me.

But just because we're two pieces in the same
puzzle,
it doesn't necessarily mean we're perfect mates.
Hell, I know better than the next guy that
every woman has her disgraces,
just like every man has his demons.

I awaken.
Same room.
Same feeling, though not as intense.
The room is no longer spinning.
The shadows and voices no longer sting me.
Gonn is gone
      and good riddance.
I need to find out what time it is.
It feels like I've been out for a fucking half hour.
I look for a clock.
Nothing is nearby.
I try to move.
A severely disorienting feeling comes over my
entire body at just the turn of my head.
Muscles twitching.
Seeing double
      or even triple at times.
I try to pull myself to my feet and fall flat on my
ass.
I try again, this time with the help of the bookshelf
behind me.

The shelves bend.
I barely get to my feet before the whole thing comes crashing to the floor.
I lean against the wall.
I'm sweating.
Breathing heavily.
It took everything in me to get to my feet.
I need the time.
I wait another minute.
Breathe.
Jesus kid, what do you see in this stuff?
Calm.
I stumble to the next room.
The clock on the wall reads 3:19 AM.
Fuck!
I've wasted damn near three and a half hours here!
FUCK!
I've got to move!
I shift my weight towards the front door but my body does not follow.
Concentrate.
I need this.
Breathe.
Every bone in this broken-down body aches.
Every time I peer out of these bloodshot eyes I see a kaleidoscope of colors with no shape.
But it's getting better.
I can *feel* it getting better.
I don't have time to wait.
Not any longer.
I need this.

Right now.
I need to do this.
I move my right foot forward.
Then my left.
I lean and crash my right shoulder into the doorway that leads into the living room.
I lean against the wall for a moment.
Already struggling to keep my breath.
Fuck.
I've got to do this.
I *must* do this.
I push away from the wall and head for the front door.
The air outside is cold and stale.
It's difficult to breathe, but then again it is difficult to do *anything* right now.
The cold air hits my lungs and fills.
I hold it in like a breath of smoke.
Sharp pains stab at my chest from all directions as I exhale.
I rest again, now on the front steps of the lopsided porch.
I breathe heavily and hold my chest as if it actually soothes the pain.
I want to die.
I don't want to go any farther.
I want to turn around and take this body right back where I found it.
I want to die.
But then I see it.
Flashes of red and blue paint the night.
They paint the buildings and the trees.

Sirens scream and follow speeding squad cars down the street in front of me.
They found it.
They found my dead body down that dark alleyway.

At first I can't help but think of how incredible it all is.
The fact that I'm seeing all of this.
After death.
I sit on that porch and stare at the red and blue flashing lights in awe.
But the feeling is short-lived.
I begin to think about what all this means for me now.
Police don't just find a dead body and leave it at that.
They investigate.
They find the killer.
In that short moment, everything changes.
It isn't about having two and a half hours to kill Ben anymore.
It's about finding Ben before the cops do.
Ben.
Just thinking of his name throws my fists in rage!
Pure white-hot rage fills my every thought!

There is nothing in this world that can stop me from getting blood on my hands tonight.

I am a broken man with dangerous thoughts.
At any given moment I fear I will kill to put an end
to my anger.
I now know the reason why people do bad things.
Why good people become savages.
Why a man would kill another man.
I now know.

I'm full of fear and hate and ash and death and
blood and rage.
Most beg for redemption.
I kill it.

I now know the reason why people hate.
Why cancer spreads.
Why winter is cold.
I now know.

I can feel the pressure of my black heart damn
near beating through my rib cage.
I want to let it out.

I kill it.

I now know the reason why terror roams free.
Why forgiveness is lost.
Why Hell burns so hot.
I now know.

Sometimes I think about Evey and she is all I
want.
And I know she is all I want.
But at any given moment, that feeling changes.
I am completely sure I love her.
I am completely sure I hate her.
I am completely sure of both of these things at
least twenty times a day.

I am a mess.
An unswept pile of ash and bone.
I miss the life before Evey.
Not always.
But now.
I miss Amy.

Scotch and water.
My only solace.
I pour myself a glass and slump down on the
couch.
I sit and stare at the nothing before me.
Evey walks into the room.
She sees me sulking in a t-shirt and robe,
unshaven, stuck on the couch,
drinking at 9 AM on a Tuesday.

She says nothing and keeps walking into the
kitchen.
Amy never would have let me get like this.
She wouldn't have allowed it.
I take another swig from my glass.

Evey walks back into the room.
She looks at the mirror.
She's fixing her earrings.
She's going out.

Where the fuck are you going?

I don't even attempt to disguise my foul mood.

What the hell is wrong with you?

I want to tell her I don't know.
That these feelings come and go
and when they're here, the weight on me is
tremendous.
I want her to hold me.
To acknowledge me.
I need her today.
I need her attention.
But she's leaving.
I want to tell her to go fuck herself.

Vincent, I'm not going to put up with your shit
today.
Just tell me where the fuck you're going.

I rub my temples.
My brain is pulsing.

I'm going out.
I can't stand being in this house any longer.
Are you going alone?

She pauses.

Actually, no...
I met this guy when I was out the other day,
I think his name is Michael,
He told me if I met with him today he would show
me his mansion on the hill.
He's a real looker, this guy, so don't wait up,
sweetie.

She's mocking me.
I say under my breath...

Evey...
What, Vincent?
Isn't that what you want to hear?
Isn't that what you want to do?
Catch me up in some hot love affair?
Fuck, Vincent, how is this supposed to work
if you don't even trust me to go to the store alone?
Goddammit, Evey.
Not today.
No, Vincent, I don't want to live like this
anymore!
I want to be comfortable with you.

MR. MALIN AND THE NIGHT

I want this to work.
You are just so fucking moody all the time!
One day I'm your queen, and the next I'm dirt
beneath your feet.
How am I supposed to feel about us when that's
all you give me?
I mean, Vincent, really... what the fuck is going
on?
You're drinking when you should be in that
garage working.
What's wrong, Vincent?
Truthfully... is it me?

She pauses.
She looks into my eyes, and I look into hers.

Is it Amy?

Even though I know she knows
what's going on with me,
I still feel pissed at the sound
of Evey saying her name.
I stand.

Evey, don't you fucking start this shit...
Well, what am I—

EVEY, DON'T YOU FUCKING START THIS SHIT!

I hurl my scotch glass toward her in a maddening
rage.
The glass shatters on the wall behind her.
It doesn't hit her,

57

but it comes close.
Too close.

You want to talk about Amy?
Okay, let's talk about Amy.

I'm staring at nothing.
Lost in thought.
Tears of anger swell in my eyes.

You want to know the truth?
The truth that's been eating at me since the day
she left?
I'll tell you.
Amy was a fucking whore!
A beautiful fucking whore,
but a whore nonetheless.
The day she left, I caught her.
In our bed.
In OUR bed, Evey!
And if you want me to be completely honest,
the reason I'm so fucking moody is because
I can see us ending that same way.
What are you saying, Vincent?

Anger burns in her eyes.

What the fuck are you saying?
I'm a whore?
Am I a fucking whore to you now?

I say nothing.

I feel wrong, but it's the truth.
I am scarred and others will suffer for it.
She slaps my face and walks out the door.
As soon as the door closes I get the sick feeling
I will never see her again.

I kick the door to Ben's house in.
No one is home.
I look through everything.
Completely destroy the place.
I want to know what the fuck is going on.
How did Ben know?
I empty every drawer onto the floor.
I turn over all of his furniture.
The only thing I find is a stack of photographs.
Many of them are of Amy.
I fall to my knees.
I feel sick...
    and this time it's not the heroin.
I know Amy and Ben were friends, but the actual thought of Ben and Amy being anything more nearly causes me to vomit.
Amy was the one for me.
I just couldn't fathom it being any different.
Looking at these pictures makes me want to do more than just murder the man.
I stick them in my back pocket.

Fuel.

As I leave, I happen to spot a notebook sitting by
the phone.
The top page is blank except for something
written in the top right-hand corner.

Evey Winters
Corner Coffee Shop
9 PM

I take the phone, throw it against the wall as hard
as I can, and walk out the door.

The only other place I know to look is back at our
house.
Maybe Evey will be there.
Maybe I can get her to tell me where Ben is hiding.
Maybe I can hear her voice one last time before I
go.
Maybe.
The road home is a long trek from here.
Too long to walk on foot.
I only have two hours now.
I'll have to find an alternate means.
Parked down the street, in the driveway of a nice
A-frame house, is a rusty old '76 El Camino.
I walk down and open the door.
With a twist of wires, the engine roars.
The old car is loud and I make no effort to try and
sneak it out quietly.
I slam on the gas and screech out of the sleeping

neighborhood.

I drive for about fifteen minutes straight, going no less than eighty miles an hour through urban streets.
I make pretty good time for the distance.
I ditch the car three blocks down from our house and walk the rest of the way.
I can't scare her off.
The cold immediately finds home in the bones of my hands.
I double my arms across my chest to keep warm and surprisingly find a half-empty pack of cigarettes stashed in the pocket of my shirt.
How thoughtful.
Shit, maybe this donor guy wasn't so bad after all.
I stop to light and inhale.
The sharp stabbing pain that resides in my chest seems to subside a bit when I fill it with smoke.
Although it returns violently as I exhale.
I start coughing.
Choking...   on smoke...
               on phlegm...
               on something thicker.
I continue coughing to clear my throat until it finally surfaces.
A sordid ball of mucus fills my mouth.
But it's not mucus.
It has a sharp metallic taste.
Thick coagulated blood flows out of my mouth and onto the ground below.
Before I get the chance to recoil, something

catches my eye.
Red.
Blue.
Red.
Blue.
Another swarm of squad cars fills the street before
my house.

Shit!

I duck down behind a nearby tree.
Shit!
Shit!
Shit!
What if they found Ben?
What if they found Evey?
I have to find out what the fuck is going on.
I take one final draw from my cigarette and toss it
onto the street.
I walk toward the house.
I can hear a muffled conversation in the distance.
I move in closer.
There are two cops standing outside of the house
talking.

...I'm telling you, the guy's brains were fucking
sprayed all over the pavement!

Jesus Christ! So what's wrong with the girl?
I heard you had to take her to St. Joe's when she
turned herself in.

Get this, she said she was holding him when she
shot him in the face.

The bullet went through his forehead and into her
shoulder!
Her boyfriend gave the same statement.

I'm getting that sick feeling in my stomach again.
Eveythatmotherfuckingbitch!
I want to grind her teeth into the pavement!
I want to empty every last drop of her blood on the
ground!
No...
I want even more...
I want to rip her soul from her body.
I want her to burn in Hell.
I want to see her suffer!

I do.

Sounds like bullshit to me. It's a cover.
That's what I thought at first,
but the evidence holds up so far.
We're still holding the guy in custody too,
just until the story officially checks out.

The cops continue babbling, but I can't concen-
trate on anything they're saying.
Only Evey. Only Evey. Only Evey.
I turn back and walk away from the house.
I'm completely fucking shocked.
Enraged.
Outraged.
Betrayed!
I need to go to St. Joseph's Hospital.

I need to find Evey.
I need to find her and I need to end her.
Evey and Ben.
They did this together,
I decide to take the metro.
That way I can think.
I can't drive with my hands shaking
the way they are now, anyway.
I walk to the station.
I don't blink.
Not even once.

Evey flew back to stay with her parents.
She's called and left three messages.
She says we need time alone.
That we need to think about what we both want
from this relationship.
She says she might not come back.
Maybe it's for the best.

I haven't answered the phone since she left [two
weeks].
Customers have been calling about their cars.
The garage is full and I haven't started working on
anything.
I just don't give a shit anymore.
I feel totally disconnected from the world.
Am I the only one disconnected?
Or are there others out there drowning
alone in pools of lament?

I pull out Amy's old vinyls.
I drink and I listen.

Amy's soul pours into my ears.
Every word, she sings to me.
I hear a song called "Green Grass" and I fall apart.
Tears swell and slide down my cheeks.

She's gone.

I dry my eyes and decide to take a late drive.
What better to do at 3 AM when my only
alternative is this empty house?
These cold November nights are starting to get to
me.
Every wintry gust of wind seems to seep in
through any and every crack in the wall to find me.
I haven't been sleeping so well lately.
I'd like to say that's the reason.

I put on my coat and head out the door.
I sift through my pockets, searching for the keys.
I find them.
I unlock the car door.
I put the key in the ignition but wait to turn it.
Hand in turning position—a memory finds me.

Her scent.
Her skin.
I can almost feel her sitting next to me.
She goes away with a turn of my head.

I turn the key.

The car barely starts.

Years before I met Evey, I was married to a girl
named Amy.
Amy was beautiful.
Perfect hair.
Perfect face.
Perfect body.
She was from Kentucky, but didn't have much of
an accent.
She had great taste in everything, too.
Our house looked like the dream homes you see in
magazines, but still comfortable enough to live in.
She wanted the world, I could taste it when we
kissed.
I miss those days when I would
come home and catch her lost in song
completely unaware of the world around her.
Sometimes I'd watch for as long as an hour before
I'd let her know I was there.
Tom Waits.
She was obsessed with the man.
Mostly the jazz stuff he did in the seventies.

Nothing was more beautiful to me than hearing her sing "Tom Traubert's Blues."
The music defined her.
Soft.
Slow.
Broken.
Beautiful.
Amy could have had anybody, but all she wanted was me, and she let me know *every day*.
And even though I knew it was only me she wanted, I still would get jealous seeing her with other men.
Amy used to get so pissed at me over it.
I had no problem beating the life out of the fucks she used to hang around with if I so much as suspected anything was happening between them.
I trusted Amy.
I did.
I just didn't trust *them*.
Anyway, Amy and I started fighting a lot.
It was like we would try and find any kind of bullshit excuse to start some shit with each other.
Even though I felt like I hated her at times, deep down I still knew I loved her.

On the last night of our marriage, I came home from work a few hours early and caught her in bed with another woman.

Vincent!

I didn't ask for her name.

I didn't ask what the fuck was going on.
I didn't say a fucking word.

Vincent?

I just walked over to the dresser where I kept my gun and blew both of them down right there in our bed.
I don't know the exact moment Amy stopped loving me, I just know that she did.
I couldn't go on living knowing she wanted to be with someone else.

Killing her was the only way to kill my anger.

Killing her was the only way I could suppress the pain.

I wrapped their naked bodies in sheets and dragged them to the back of the house.
This house...
    our house...
        used to be Amy's grandparent's house.
When they passed away they left it to us.
They asked to be buried in the family graveyard, behind the house, where they had laid to rest their brothers and sisters before them.
The first thing that came to mind as I was trying to hide the bodies was to bury them there.
Amy would have wanted it.
I didn't give a fuck what Jane Doe wanted.
After I buried the girls, I cleaned up the bedroom and took a shower.
I thought about what to do.
Should I turn myself in?
Should I run?
Either way, I was going to live with the guilt.
So I stayed.
If I got caught, I got caught.
But luckily for me, Amy didn't keep in touch with her parents,
or really anyone for that matter.
The only family she ever spoke of were her grandparents, and they were dead.
No one called for her.
She didn't have a job.
Her friends were all too afraid to call the house.

I sat in the house for three more months before I got up the nerve to report her missing.

I made up some bullshit story about her leaving after an argument.
I threw out most of her stuff over time to make it seem like she packed up and left.
The cops didn't seem suspicious of foul play.
The graves had already grown a thick head of grass.
Their bodies were but soil.
During the investigation, detectives found the rest of her family and told them Amy was missing.
Her parents flew in to see me.
They wanted to know everything.
The last thing she said.
The *argument*.
What she had been doing in the years they hadn't spoken.
They believed me.
They gave me Amy's sister's phone number.

> *She'll want to know everything too.*
> *She's just being stubborn.*
> *She'll listen to you.*
> *Please, Vincent.*

It turns out when Amy left the family,
her sister took it hard.
Harder than the rest of them.
Amy was as good as dead to her.
I guess that's why Amy never even mentioned having a sister to me before.
Her parents said when they phoned her up to tell her that her sister was missing, she didn't seem

affected by it in the slightest.
It scared them.
That's why they wanted me to call her.
They knew deep inside she cared.
At least they hoped she did.
So, later that week I called.

Hello?
Uh... hi, is this Evey Winters?
Who is this?
Vincent Malin. Your sister's husband.
What the fuck do you want?
Your parents asked me to call you.
Well, I don't have a fucking sister. You must have
the wrong number.

And she hung up.
Two days later the phone rings.
Evey is crying so hard she can barely speak.
I calm her down and we talk.
We talk for hours about Amy.
About our marriage.
About their childhood.
About the "fight."
Everything.
Before we got off of the phone that night, Evey had already ordered a plane ticket to come and stay with me the following morning.
Evey wanted to see her sister's house,
to meet me,
and wait for Amy to call.
Of course, that call never came, but in the

meantime Evey and I became comfortable living
with each other.
One night we were sitting on the couch watching a
movie and something she saw struck a nerve.
She lost total control.
She cried as I held her.
To this day I still don't know what it was that
made her cry, but I was sure it was over Amy.
I held her all night.
She kissed me and for the first time since Amy's
death I felt *that feel*.
The next day we said nothing of the kiss.
In fact, we did nothing out of the ordinary at all.
But that night, when I went to bed, Evey followed.

> *Can I sleep in here with you tonight?*
> Wherever you're comfortable, Evey.
> You know that.

She took off her clothes and lay next to me.
She put her arms around me and kissed my chest.
Kissed my chin.
Kissed my lips.
We kissed and held each other close all night.
Nothing more.
Evey and I were both a fucked up mess of
emotions, and we both respected that.
It wasn't right what we were doing.
We had already gone too far and we knew it.
But goddammit, I was falling for her the same way
I had fallen for her sister years before.
They were practically the same person.

They were similar not only physically, but mentally.

So similar, in fact, that in the beginning I would often mistakenly call her Amy.

She never corrected me, but I could see it in her eyes that it bothered her.

Of course it bothered her.

She decided to get a job working part-time as a waitress.

She did it just to get out of the house, I'm guessing, 'cause my garage had been pulling in more than enough to cover the bills.

Eventually, Evey felt comfortable enough with me that she started introducing me as her boyfriend.

We used to argue about what would happen if Amy were to return.

Evey was so insecure.

She always felt as if she'd been living in her sister's shadow.

She was wrong.

She needed someone to blame for her pain.

Hell, everyone does.

Anyway, I knew the moment the bullet pierced through my brain that I deserved the hand I was dealt.

I knew my day was coming sooner rather than later,

but I still can't say I'm not shocked at how it all went down.

Evey.

Fuck!
No matter how right it may seem for me to die and
for this to be my end, I still feel the need to kill.
I still feel the need to seek vengeance.
I'm sick, I know.
Always have been.

I know one thing for damn sure,
I'm not walking into Hell alone tonight.

I had that fucking dream again last night.
The one where I'm stuck inside an empty room
with no doors or windows.
My dead wife is lying propped up in the corner,
opposite of me.
All she does is stare at me.
She's dead, but still she stares at me.
The strangest thing about it is how comfortable I
am staring back at her.
I don't even panic at knowing there's no apparent
way out of the room.
I'm not frightened.
Never scared.
I tell her I miss her.
She just stares back at me.
Sometimes I touch her.
Most of the time, I don't.
Whatever I do, it always ends the same.

She smiles,
vaguely.

And all the fury buried deep within starts to pour
out of me
onto the floor below.
So enraged I can't control my hands…
!!!
So enraged I can't control my mind…
!!!
So enraged I rip off her rotted jawbone and break
her teeth against the wall.

It always ends the same.

Always.

Why the fuck am I never alone
with my thoughts?
Why the fuck do I keep *myself* out?
Why the fuck?

In everything I do, I try to see the purpose.
I try to see the life within.
I try to make it something.
But my mind has soured lately.
I can't seem to keep thoughts on the shelf.
My eyes get blacker with every sunset and
I wonder if my heart still bleeds the same.

Why does her body haunt me so [AMY]?
Why is it *her* in my head
night after night
tearing through everything that keeps me stable?
Why is it her?

This woman?
Why does she always come *to me*?

I'm so clouded right now.
I know I'm not making any sense.
I'm just surprised, I guess
At how fucked up I *really* am.
At how naturally these feelings come to me now.
At how fucked up it is for me to feel comfortable
with all of this.
With desecrating my dead wife's remains.
With ripping off her jawbone and laughing at how
far her teeth scatter when it shatters against the
wall.
I'm just surprised
At how I seem to be so normal
to everyone else.

I need Evey.
I call.

> *Hello?*
> Hey babe...
> it's me.
> *Vincent... what's wrong?*

Two weeks of guilt and tears have formed a lump
in my throat.
I speak slowly.

> I need you.
> Will you please come home?

Vincent, it's not that easy—
I know, I know...
We have problems,
everybody has problems,
but being apart isn't helping any.
I miss you.
I need you, Evey.

I can hear a nervous quiver in Evey's voice.

Vincent... you really hurt me.
I don't know if I could come back to you
with the things you said to me that day.
I know.
I'm sorry.
I've been a complete asshole and I'm sorry.

Something is wrong with me.
I need help.
I never know what I want or even need,
but I do know in this exact moment, it is her that I
want.
She is the only thing that can calm my nerves
and put me at ease.

I need you, Evey.
I need you here with me tonight.
Tonight?
Vincent... I miss you too,
but you know that I can't be there tonight.
It's impossible.

We talked for exactly thirty-three minutes.
At the end of the call she told me she was going
to check the next available flight,
    without any promises.
She was home by dawn the next day.

The seats on the metro seem to have been installed backwards.
They are awkward and uncomfortable.
The air smells heavy of vomit and urine
and the lights flicker on and off at any given moment.

One hour of life left and this is where I choose to be.

There is only one other person sharing this joy ride with me tonight.
A drunken hobo who got on two stops after me.
When I first saw him sitting on the bench outside the train, I thought he was dead.
There was no movement in his body.
His lips were blue.
It seemed an act of fate that he even made it *onto* the train.
His eyes opened only seconds before the doors closed.

He staggered to his feet and sprinted just in time
to have the doors pinch shut against his right arm
and foot.

Goddamntrainmother...

He spoke slow and slurred, yet in a calm tone that
made it seem like this is a fairly common situa-
tion for him.
He pulled his arm and foot into the railcar just
before it took off.
With nearly the entire train empty, he slumped
down in the seat directly opposite of me.
Of course he did.
He passed out again almost immediately.

He's a pretty big guy for a bum.
I mean, I guess he manages to eat well.
He's wearing a long executive-style trench coat.
It would be a nice jacket on anyone else.
On him, it looks like devastation.

I try to figure out his story.
What brought him here tonight?
What caused this?
Of all the places in the world, why is his ass sitting
here on this train?
How did it come to be that this is the only place he
has left to go?
What went wrong?

The lights flicker off again.

Darkness.
My whole life summed up in just one word.
The lights flicker and turn back on and the bum is
staring straight at me.

Whatthefuckyoulookingat,boy?

I look away.
I don't have time for trouble.
Shit.
He's getting up.
Shit.
Shit.

Answerme,boy!Whatthefuckyoulookingat?

He's walking towards me now.
He sticks his fat finger in my face
and my anger gets the best of me.
I grab his hand and throw it back at him.
I stare him down.
Anger fills his glassy pink eyes.

Youjustmadethebiggestmistakeofyourlife,asshole!

He lunges at me.
I duck under and hit him in his lower back.
He tumbles over, swearing.
He pulls himself up to his feet.

You'regonnadie,motherfucker!

He swings his arm like a hammer drilling a spike,
     but falls short.
About a *foot* short.
The man is dead drunk.
He loses his footing and, by luck, pins me against
the wall of the train.
He grabs hold of me with one arm and starts
pumping his other into my gut like some sort of
machine.
He knocks the wind clear out of me.
I'm struggling to breathe, and he continues to beat
wildly at my ribcage.
I can't do anything in this weak fucking body.
I feel helpless.
He rises up and grabs my throat.
He's choking me.
I gasp for air.
He beats my face with his fist.
I can feel the blood pouring down from my eyes,
my nose,
my mouth.
I can feel it.
This is it.
Being beaten to death by a drunk hobo on the
metro.
Another surprise ending.
But then he stops.
I look up at him.
Puzzled.
He says nothing.
He doesn't even look angry anymore,
or drunk for that matter.

He steps back,
away from me.
He pulls out a small bottle of Maker's Mark from
his inside coat pocket.
Pulls off the cap.
Pours the contents onto the floor.
I stare in pure terror.
He takes the top of the bottle in his hand and
smashes the end on a seat.
Glass shatters and scatters.
In his hands, he holds the shard remains of the
bottleneck.
He continues staring blankly.
No words.
He holds the jagged glass chest high.
I wait.
Terrified.
I wait.
He moves suddenly.
I flinch.
Blood sprays and spatters.
He is jamming the glass into his own neck.
He does this repeatedly.
The blood leaves his body in violent flight.
I scream out.

WHAT THE FUCK? JESUS GOD!

He falls to the floor in a pool of his own blood.
It's silent now.
All I can do is shake and stare.

MR. MALIN AND THE NIGHT

Get the fuck up.

Gonn.
He is standing now over the dead body.
He looks at me.

This is your stop, Mr. Malin.

The train stops.
I'm bleeding.
My face is swollen in pain.
I think a rib or two may be broken.
The night seems impossible to complete.
I walk to the doors and step out onto the
pavement.
The hospital is directly above me now.
All I have to do is walk up those stairs and I'm
there.
Evey is only stories away now.

Slowly, I make it up the stairs and to the street.
As I reach for the hospital doors, a church bell
rings.
It's 5:30.
I have half an hour left.
I turn around and walk into the church.
The pews are empty.
It's dark.
Warm.
A statue of Jesus hanging on the cross
stands before me.
I stare into his eyes.

After a moment, I speak.

    Look, I didn't come here to ask for forgiveness...

I find it hard to speak in church.
A weight pulls at my throat.
It's difficult, but I manage.

        The Devil's had a hold of me since the day I was
                  born
          and I've come here to confess.
          I wanted to tell you myself
            I know I've done wrong.
            I know I deserve this.
              This fate.
              This doom.

                I know.

I try to keep silent.
To fight the tears.
I bite my lower lip.

        I've sinned time and time again, Lord.
          And after this last sin,
         I'll go to Hell for them all.
           And I deserve this.
             I know.
         All I ask of you is to
           hold me.
        Just hold me as I fall.

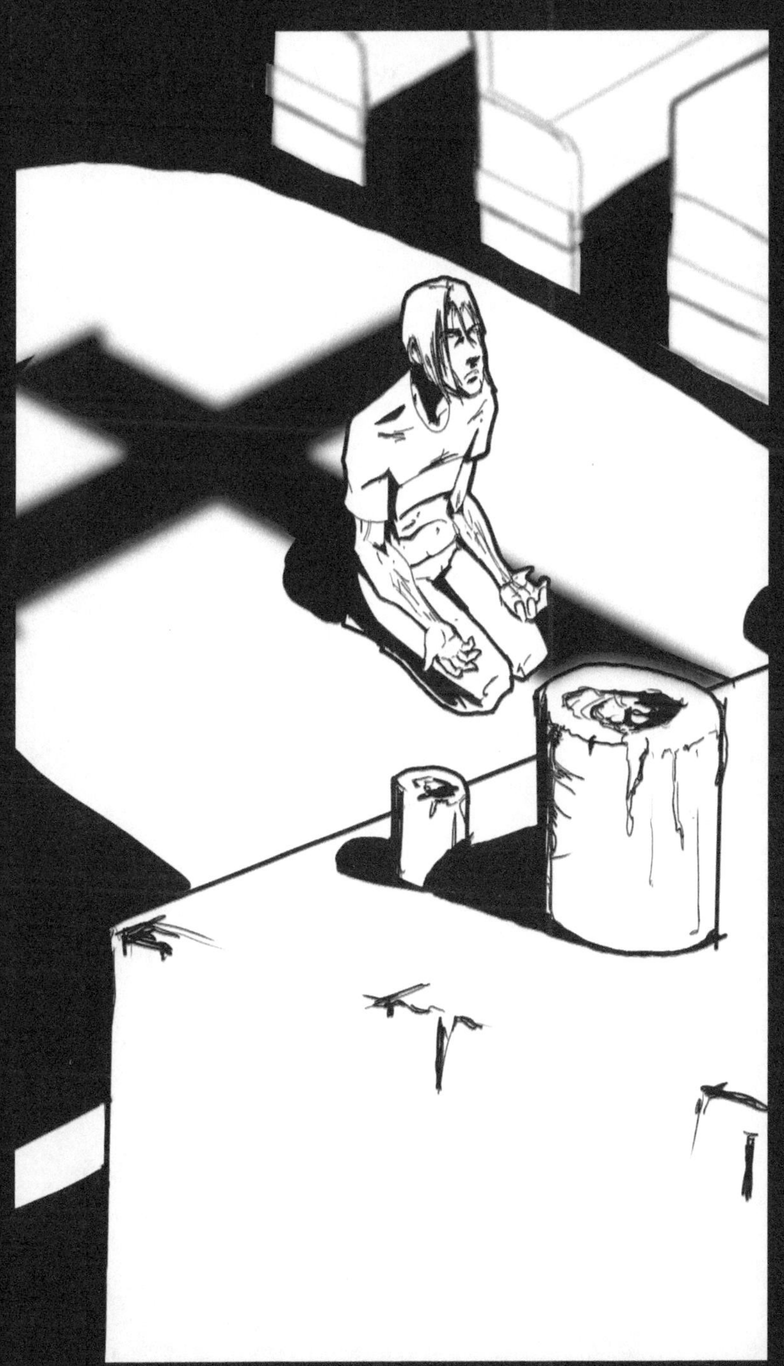

Will you do that for me?

The tears come now.
I'm sobbing.
Sitting in this silent church.
Waiting for an answer
that never comes.

Evey hasn't been the same since she's returned.
I can't tell if she's suspicious or cautious,
but there's definitely something wrong here.
She's different.
She's colder.
The only night we've slept together was the night
she flew back.
She says she's having trouble sleeping,
but I think she's figuring things out on her own.

I never should have told her about Amy fucking
around on me.
Now she knows there's *more* to the story.
That I would hide something from her.
She's putting the puzzle together one piece at a
time.
And it changes *everything* in her mind.
About me.
About Amy.
About the fact her sister hasn't been seen or heard
from in over three months.

She has to be suspicious.
She must.
She's not sure, or she'd be gone.
But she's afraid.
I can see it in her eyes.

I know I should be worried about the things she
knows.
I should be nervous.
I should be sick.

But I'm not.

Possibly because I've been drinking,
but likely because I feel I'm ready to face these
demons.
I've lived with Amy's ghost for damn near a year
now.
I'm ready to let go.
To be free.
If it was only that easy.

The only thing I regret is Evey.
I never should have let it come to this.
I love her.
Tears cloud my eyes.
Fuck this.
Alcohol always turns me into a fucking sad
bastard.
Truth is, I'm not a man who sits around and waits
for things to happen.
I seek it out.

I want to know.
Is she cheating on me?
Is she digging up my past?
Why the fuck is she so spent?
I need to know.
When Evey leaves tonight, I'm following her.

I load my 9mm.
Just in case.

As I walk through the front doors of the emergency room, the smell hits me.
Sickness.
Death.
There's a woman screaming to my right.
A nurse tries to calm her.
There's a woman who claims her baby has been waiting to be
seen by a doctor for over five hours.
Tears well in her eyes.
The woman at the front desk apologizes and tells her they are understaffed and they are treating people as quickly as they can.
The room is packed to capacity.
Some have to stand because there aren't enough seats.
The news is playing on every television in the room.
As if the scene wasn't depressing enough already.

I walk up to the woman at the front desk.

She doesn't seem to be shocked by my appearance.

Sign in here, sir.

She hands me a clipboard with pages stacked half
an inch thick,
folds over to the last page where there is barely
enough room for me to write my name.
I look up at her.
She sighs and offers me a pen.

Actually, I am visiting a friend.

She just stares.

Sir, you're clearly in need of medical attention.
I'll be fine. I just need to see my friend.
*Sir, I can't allow you to walk through
the premises in your condition.*
I told you, I'll be f—
SIR!

A security guard standing by the door makes it
known to me he is watching.
He cracks his knuckles as a silent threat.
What a fucking putz.
I lean over the desk and whisper.

Please, it's important.
*I just need to find out what room my friend is in
and I'll be on my way.*

She says nothing.
I feel the security guard's hand on my shoulder.
I don't have time for this shit.
I need to find Evey.
There are other ways to do this.
I turn around and walk out the doors.
I find a payphone outside,
pick up the receiver, and dial information.

St. Joseph's Hospital, please.

The operator puts me through.
The same woman sitting at the front desk answers.
I am watching her through the glass front doors.

Thank you for calling St. Joseph's Hospital.
How may I help you?

I talk an octave lower than my normal speaking
voice.

Uh, yes... I was just looking for my daughter,
her name is Evey Winters.
I believe she's been shot.
I need to see her right away.
What room is she in?

Silence.

Winters...
Winters...
Ah yes, Evey Winters.

Room 3111.
But sir, that room has been flagged as being
under high security,
we cannot allow visitors at this t—

I hang up the phone.
Room 3111.

I enter through the side entrance of the hospital.
There is no one in sight.
The hospital is colder than the night air outside,
But despite that, it feels like a comfortable place.
It's a shame so many people come to die here.

I find an elevator.
I push the up button and it glows a pale yellow.
The doors open.
There's a small elderly lady standing before me.
She has a look of terror on her face.
I must look like I just walked out of a fucking freak accident.
I step into the elevator and the doors close behind me.
As we lift to the third floor, the elderly woman slowly greatens the distance between us.
When the doors open, I glance back at her.
She is in the farthest corner away from me with her back turned.
She looks like a child being punished.
I turn away and walk out onto the third floor.
I walk down the hall and follow the room numbers to Evey's.

3107.

3109.

3111.

This is it.

There is a police officer down the hall flirting with one of the nurses.
My guess would be that he's supposed to be guarding *this* door.
Evey's door.
Number 3111.

The door I am walking through now.

I drive out to the garage.
Not for work,
       for a car.
I can't follow Evey in mine.
Too suspicious.
Besides, there's an old Sting Ray out here I've been
wanting an excuse to drive.
The owner brought it in because it was "shaking
violently" in certain gears.
It turns out it was just a bad spark plug.
Of course, I made up some bullshit story and
charged three times as much for a job I didn't even
do.
It only seemed right to me.
A man as ignorant as that shouldn't be allowed to
own a car this classic.
I get in.
The engine roars.

It's a goddamn sin.

I drive it back to our neighborhood and park a
block from our house.
I can see Evey's car in the driveway.
It's starting to get dark.
I can tell what she's doing just by watching the
shadows in the windows.
She's in the bathroom.
She's taking a shower.
The heat fogs the glass.
After about twenty minutes she moves to the
bedroom.
Clothes.
Make-up.
Lights out.
The lights go out long enough for me to think
maybe she isn't going out tonight.
I almost leave when the front door opens.
Half her face is illuminated a pale blue.
She's on the phone.
My blood starts boiling.

Caughtcha!
Come on...
Take me to him, Evey!

She gets in her car and starts it up.
The lights shine bright on the front of the house.
She sits... and waits.
She hangs up her phone and tosses it in her purse.
Her reverse lights come on and
she pulls out onto the street.
I give her plenty of lead before I start my car and

follow.
I catch up to her two blocks down where she's
stuck at a traffic light.
I'm about two cars behind.
I intend to keep this distance.

Evey pulls up to an old diner located on the
corner of a slummy hotel parking lot.
Business must be slow, because there are
only two other cars in the lot.
I park by the curb across the street
from the diner.
I turn the engine off.
She's sitting there.
She's waiting for someone.
Only minutes go by before another car
pulls up beside her.
A baby blue pacer.
Evey steps out of her car.
I try to control my anger.
Watching her.
Wondering who it is she is sneaking off and
seeing.
I grip the steering wheel so hard my knuckles turn
white.
Come on.
Come on, motherfucker...
Get out of the car.
The car door opens.
A body steps out.
It's a man.
I punch the dashboard and get out of the car.

I walk across the street enraged.
They are standing there in the parking lot talking.
Evey is the first to see me approaching, but by the
time she realizes who I am, I'm only ten feet away.

Oh shit, it's Vincent.

She warns the man.
He turns around.
To my surprise, the face attached is a face I recog-
nize.
It's Ben... I can't remember his last name.
He was an old friend of Amy's.
The wind suddenly gets colder.
Evey isn't here to cheat on me.
She is here to investigate.

Vincent, it's not what it looks like...

I can't look at her.

I know.

I look over at Ben.

This is about Amy.

Ben keeps quiet.
Shifting his eyes from me to Evey.
He's intimidated by me.
He's one of those fucks that Amy and I
used to fight about.

I knew there was nothing going on between them.
I just wanted her all to myself.
I stare into his eyes.
I can smell the fear rolling off him.
Evey distracts me from Ben.

> *I asked Ben to come out here so I could find out*
> *more about Amy.*
> *You're right, Vincent.*
> *I need to know more about my sister.*

I wish that's all it was, but I can see it in Evey's
eyes—she knows.
I can see she's afraid of me.
I can see she's scared.
I can see why she's kept her distance from me.

> Cut the shit, Evey.
> I know why he's here.
> I know why you're here.
> I know you know!
> I know what the fuck is going on here!
> So cut the shit!

I light a cigarette.
As I return the lighter to my jacket pocket, I trace
the outline of my 9mm with my index finger.
I glance at the diner behind Evey.
The customers and employees sense trouble
brewing.
They're watching us with suspicious eyes.
We need to get out of here before the cops are

called.

Here, come with me.

I motion toward an alleyway half a block down.
Ben follows.
Evey stays.
She's afraid.
She knows what will happen if we leave.

Come on, Evey!
They're going to call the cops!
I don't give a shit, Vincent!
I don't have anything to hide!

I start to speak, but Ben interrupts.

It's okay, Evey.
Let's go.

It's strange.
Now that I think of it, I've never heard Ben speak before tonight.
I guess it's the whole intimidation thing.
His voice doesn't sound the way I was expecting it to sound.
Evey follows closely behind Ben, all the while keeping a watchful eye on every move I make.
We walk down the alley.
I reach for the gun.
As soon as I lift my hand, Ben pulls out a gun and aims it between my eyes.

> *Put down the gun, Vincent!*
> What gun?
> *PUT THE FUCKING GUN ON THE GROUND*
> *OR I'M GOING TO BLOW YOUR FUCKING*
> *BRAINS OUT!*

I knew it wouldn't work, but I thought I'd at least try.
I take the gun out of my jacket pocket and slowly place it on the ground before me.
A higher power is behind all this.
It isn't Ben holding the gun tonight.
It is the Devil.
It is God.
It is something bigger than man.
They found me.
And tonight, there's no escaping their judgment.

There's a rubber wedge on the floor used to hold open doors.
I use the wedge to do the exact opposite, to make sure the door stays shut.

To my surprise, Evey's not lying on the bed, she's in the shower.
I walk into the bathroom, steam billowing out, and peek behind the curtain.
It's her.
She has large bandages taped to the front and back of her left shoulder.
She's trying not to get them wet.
She looks distraught.
Her face is swollen.
I can tell she's been crying.
She twists the knobs and the water turns off.
She reaches for a towel and dries herself.

I start to shake.
Remembering Amy.

Remembering Evey.
Remembering how difficult it was to get here tonight.
Remembering Gonn.
Remembering the bum on the subway.
Remembering all the pain.
        all the suffering.
        all the hurt.
Evey murdered me.
She ended my life.
My anger shivers.
Rage!
Pure rage!
Pure fucking rage flows through my bloodless veins!
I want to see her suffer.
I want to see her in pain!
The worst fucking pain one could ever experience.
We are going to Hell tonight hand-in-hand!

Evey stands in front of a steamed mirror.
Droplets of condensation collect and stream.
Each stream captures a finite glimpse of Evey's body.
Four bright bulbs burn above.
She has a white towel wrapped around her naked body.
Hair drips wet.
She reaches out to wipe the mirror clean.

                         FUCK!

She shrieks at the image of the donor's face, just
behind hers, watching her.
His bloody broken junkie-fucked face.
She nearly jumps out of her skin.

WHAT THE FUCK?

She turns around and steps back so fast she loses
her balance and topples to the floor.

Eeeevvvvveeeyyyyy...

I say in a low whisper.
She screams again.
Crying now, she grabs the small metal trash can
beside the toilet.
She curses at me and slings it with all her might.
She misses.
The mirror shatters into a sea of splintered glass.

WHO THE FUCK ARE YOU?
WHAT DO YOU WANT?

I lean close to her left ear.

Was there ever a better time?
Evey, your heart is as black as mine.

She's shaking.
She's crying.
She whispers.

MR. MALIN AND THE NIGHT

Vincent? How?

She's sobbing now.
Trying to understand what is happening.

Vincent... Jesus, please!

I leave the donor's body and it falls to the floor.
I take hold of Evey's bones and pull myself inside
of her.
I can feel her skin tighten around me.
I feel life again.
Pure life, unsullied by drugs.
It feels great...

for a moment.

I pull Evey's body to her feet.
Walk forward two steps.
Shards of glass slice into her feet like hot butter.
It stings.
I can feel everything she's feeling.
She's terrified.
I speak, but with her voice.

You're lost.

I'm lost.

But in the end... will it even matter?

I take Evey's hand and pick up a piece of mirror,
the size of a dagger.
I hold it against her left ear.
The sharp end pushes just enough to not break the
skin.

In the end...

I push deep into her flesh.
I can feel the shard scrape against bone.
I pull down and slowly trace her jawline.
She's screaming inside.
I can feel it.
I pull down to her chin and trace up the other side.
Evey, you fucking bitch.
I jerk the shard quickly, tearing the flesh of her
face up on the side of her cheek.
She's horrified.
She's screaming bloody murder.

She deserves this.
She murdered me.
She took everything from me.
She deserves this.

I set the sliver of bloody mirror down on the
blood-spattered countertop.
Evey's white towel is now deep red at the top.
Her face is leaking streams of blood, faster by the
second.

I take her hand and dig the fingers beneath the tear in the right
side of her face.
Blood gushes down her hand and slithers along her arm.
With a quick pull, I remove the skin at the bottom of her face, clear from her
skull.
Inside, she never stops screaming.
It feeds me.

She deserves this.

I grab the loose bits of torn skin in a fist and pull towards the ceiling, exposing the bloody muscles of her jaws and mouth.
I pull harder.
The cartilage in her nose rips easier than I had expected it to.
Blood pours down her neck and shoulders.
The blood pours faster now.
Her white towel has soaked up so much blood it can't absorb another drop.
I can feel it running down her legs now...
    to her ankles...
        to the floor below.
I tug again at her skin.
This time it rips all the way to the top of her forehead.
Her eyeballs are exposed completely now.
Those beautiful fucking blue eyes.
I wouldn't *dare* touch them.

I reach for the bloody shard of mirror again.
I cut the last few inches of skin that connects her
face to her scalp until it
is severed completely.
She's screaming.
She's crying.
She's sobbing.
She's terrified.
She's horrified.

She's a monster.

I leave her body and watch as she regains control.
Her screams resound with full force.

Six minutes.
I only have six more minutes left before she must
die.
And she must kill *herself*.
All I can do is wait.
                    wait.
                       wait.

A crowd has gathered behind the front door,
hearing her screams, but unable to get to her
because of the jam.
They break down the door.
A flood of police officers, doctors, and nurses spill
through the room and cover Evey and the donor.
Evey, still screaming, can't even begin to explain
what just happened.

I have failed.
Evey is not going to die tonight.
If anything, she will be restrained.
She'll be taken to emergency surgery
to reattach her face
she'll have scars to remind her of me
for the rest of her life
but she will not die tonight.
She will never be free.
She may even kill herself over it... eventually.
But she will not die tonight.

And that's when I see it.
That's when I see she's not a monster.
I'm a monster.
I'm a fucking demon from Hell.

Time's up.

Evey stands behind Ben.
She's been crying since Ben pulled out the gun.
I try to calm her.

                              Evey, it's okay, baby.

She wipes the tears from her eyes.
Her face burns red with anger.

  What the fuck do you mean everything is okay?
          You murdered my fucking sister, Vincent!

The way she looked when she said it, I knew Evey
wasn't completely sure what she had just said was
true.
I'm the only one who knows what happened that
night,
but I don't deny it.
I can't look at her like this and lie anymore.
I hang down my head.
Evey screams.

I look up at her and see her coming at me.

Goddammit, Vincent!

Tears flowing like a stream down
both sides of her face.
She punches me in the gut.
The shoulders.
My face.
She knocks the wind from me.
I don't make any effort to try and stop her.
I know I deserve this.
I deserve more punishment than this.

She stops and holds her head in her hands.
She's crying uncontrollably now.
She's shaking and having trouble breathing.
I look over at Ben.
He's still standing with his gun pointed directly at
me.
He hasn't taken his eyes away from the target.

Evey, you have to understand.
I never wanted to hurt her.
I loved her.
I just didn't know what to do.
I was blind with rage!
You could never understand that feeling until it's
happened to you.

She looks so fucking scared.
I'm going to lose her.

She isn't coming near.
COME TO ME, GODDAMMIT!

V i N c e N T...

She's crying so hard now, I can barely understand
her.
I'm going to lose her.

Come to me.

Baby, calm down.
I'm here.
I'm the same man you've always known.
I just need you.
Damn it, Evey. Please!

I reach out my hand.
Come to me.

P l e a s e...

She falls to her knees.
I'm losing her.
I walk towards her, keeping an eye on Ben.
His gun follows every move I make.
I'm close now.
He looks nervous.
I know he doesn't want to shoot,
but I also know he will.

Ben.
You know I love her, man.
Please. Give me a minute.
I'm not going to hurt her.
You know this…
please.
You touch her and you're dead.
GODDAMMIT! GIVE ME ONE FUCKING
MINUTE WITH HER!
*Vincent, one more move and you're a fucking
dead man!*

Goddammit!
I'm so fucking close to her!
I could reach out and touch her, I'm so close!
I just need a minute!
She is kneeling on the wet pavement.
Head in hands.
Sobbing.
Poor beautiful Evey.
All I need is one fucking minute!

Just then, Evey reaches out and pulls me to her.
She pulls so hard I fall to the ground.
Still sobbing.
She doesn't even try to speak.
She just holds me tight.
I move to try and hold her, but she won't let me.
She is holding me so tight.
My head is lying on her chest.
I can hear her heartbeat.
I love this woman.

Why the fuck did I let it come to this?
Why the fuck do these demons haunt me?
I need this woman.
I turn my head to look over Evey's shoulder.
Ben is still standing.
Gun in hand.
A fucking statue.
He says nothing.
I say nothing.
I turn my head back toward Evey.
Her breathing stops.
Her eyes open wide.
She murders me.
Those eyes.
That stare.
Her heartbeat is growing faster and faster.
She kills me.
Evey.
She kills me with those eyes.
That stare.
I close my eyes and bury my face in her chest.
I try to yell.
Gunshot interrupts.
Evey and I fall.
Our backs to the ground.
She's been shot in the chest.
Blood pulsing and flowing out onto the street.
She's not moving.
Those eyes.
I was dead before the bullet left the gun.
Our bodies lie still.

Blink.
Bullet.
Black.

At exactly 6 AM I realize I'm just a pawn in
Gonn's vicious game.
He never answered me before,
    but he's most certainly the Devil.
Gonn clouded every rational thought.
He threw fuel on the fire.
He wanted to see me suffer.
To see *her* suffer.
The heroin.
The cops.
The bum.
Poor, beautiful Evey.
Innocent.
It was all a part of his plan.
I'm ashamed of myself.
Of my actions.
I deserved to die in that cold, dark alley.
Ben was right to pull the trigger.
I deserved to die.
I deserved to die.
I cut her fucking face off.

I deserved to die.

It is 6:05 AM now.
Gonn still isn't here.
This is all a part of his plan.
He wants me here.
He wants me to see this.
He wants me to watch her bleed and scream and
squirm and hurt.
He wants me to see what will happen to her.
This is my Hell.
To watch her suffer.
Not only now, but the rest of her life.
I will have to watch her live the rest of her life
carrying *my* scars.

I'm watching as the doctors and nurses frantically
try to sew Evey's face back on.
They think she did this to herself.
She has the cuts on her hands to prove it.
They can't quite explain the donor's body lying on
the floor, though, but they won't have to.
They have enough proof to provide an answer.
The rest will remain a mystery.

I hear a doctor talking to the police officer
outside the door.
He tells him the wounds were self-inflicted.
He takes it down in a police report.
It's apparent that Evey will be spending the rest of
her life institutionalized.
They think she's insane.

And I must watch it all.
Her struggle.
Her torment.
With no contact.
With no apologies.
Just my empty fucking soul
chasing after Evey's.
Her
    scarred
        tortured
           broken-down
                soul.

For the rest of her life.
Maybe longer.

This is my Hell.

Dear Evey,

All thoughts were lost in the night.
The devil had a hold of these bones and I played
his puppet tonight.
I'm sorry,
if only these words could heal your many wounds.

Just so you know, even though your boots seem
bolted to the ground,
you can still stand.
Your laces may be tight,
but they can still be loosened.
Your chains may be heavy,
but your feet are still freer than free.
I love you.
You see. I see.
You are me.

Goodnight, Evey. Goodnight.

GABBY vs. WILLIEZ

Gabino Iglesias Interviews William Pauley III

Your name popped up very soon after I started reading bizarro. Looking back, that was weird because A) you're not an Eraserhead Press author, and B) your work could easily be called New Weird, strange sci-fi or something else. In a way, you somehow managed to position yourself as a force in the genre. How did that happen? How did you become one of the recognizable names early on?

For as long as people have been writing, there's been bizarro fiction. It wasn't called that initially, however, so once that type of writing was officially labeled 'bizarro,' there came some confusion.

Eraserhead Press started labeling their books as 'bizarro books,' so when people came across them they thought the definition of bizarro fiction was simply an Eraserhead Press-style book (i.e. humorous, cartoon-ish, parodies, etc). Some (most?) readers and writers still think that. Bizarro fiction is much more than goofy toilet humor written for teenagers, although admittedly at least 95% of the books labeled 'bizarro' are exactly that. I'm not trying to dismiss those works, I'm just attempting to explain why so many people might be confused as to why I'm labeled a bizarro writer when my writing doesn't seem to fit that mold. Bizarro is exploring the roads never travelled. Take a genre, or any combination of genres, and push the story past the edge, into the darkness, and find the characters living within those spaces. Breathe life into those outcasts, those weirdos and give them purpose, and a world in which they can thrive. If you do it right, you will have created something special, a completely new story, totally unique from anything anyone else has ever done in writing before. Bizarros are the extraordinary. Each and every one of us are trail-blazers.

Stepping back for a second, to their credit, Eraserhead Press tried to avoid confusion in the beginning, often saying bizarro was the literary equivalent of the cult section in a video store and/or books that could have been written by Lynch, Cronenberg, Jodorowsky, and other directors of bizarre films—despite almost none of their books fitting the latter half of that description. The confusion is there because they are selling more books and have a bigger presence than other publishers labeling their books 'bizarro,' so that's the style of book people envision when hearing the term bizarro.

Though I've personally never published through Eraserhead, my books are most certainly bizarro fiction. It's true I don't write the types of books Eraserhead would ever publish, but it would be false to say my books wouldn't be right at home in the cult section of any type of entertainment store. In fact, this book, *Mr. Malin and the Night*, may be the closest thing to a mainstream horror tale I've written, but even still, I would never expect anyone to describe it without at least using the word 'weird.'

That's the long answer, I suppose. The short answer would be that I did some artwork for Jordan Krall many years ago (for both *King Scratch* and *Beyond the Valley of the Apocalypse Donkeys*) and he very generously agreed to read a manuscript of mine, *Doom Magnetic!*, and liked it enough to give me a blurb and my first foot inside the bizarro fiction door. That, and meeting Andersen Prunty in a bookstore in Massilon, OH about 6 or 7 years ago, who would eventually publish *The Brothers Crunk* and *Hearers of the Constant Hum* on his amazing Grindhouse Press label (which at the time barely existed, with only one book published), directly contributed to my association with the bizarro genre. I owe a lot to both Jordan and Andy for their support in the beginning of my writing career.

In those seven years, you've somehow managed to create a recognizable WP3 mythos. I'm not saying you don't do work outside of it, but a lot of your work belongs to the same universe. Was this intentional? Also, it looks like some of your earliest work is gonna be making a comeback. Are

you revising it? How has your writing changed in the last half decade?

Initially, I didn't realize my stories took place within the same universe. The world of *Mr. Malin and the Night* felt very different from the world of *If You Don't Sleep, You Don't Dream*. It wasn't until after I wrote the first *Doom Magnetic!*, and while writing *The Brothers Crunk*, that I realized these characters all shared the same world. It's become a timeline, a currently sloppy and somewhat confusing timeline, admittedly, but a timeline all the same. *Malin, Hearers*, and the stories found within *Automated Daydreaming* (forthcoming) all happened before the events in *Doom Magnetic!* and *The Brothers Crunk*. There's a story or two missing from the middle that one day will be written. The Crunks transferring from the dimension found in former stories over to the dimension found in latter stories has yet to be revealed. It will happen at some point though, and it will be really fucking weird... and fun.

My first two novellas were completely overlooked when they were first published. It wasn't that they were bad—or else I wouldn't have bothered Carrion Blue with this rerelease—it was just that I was a new writer who knew almost nothing about publishing, or even writing for that matter. I was a complete nobody, and because of that, the books were only read by a handful of readers. I was just too naive at the time. I've always been a reader and have always surrounded myself with books, but that was the extent of my knowledge with writing/publishing in those days. Since writing those novellas, however, I've taken writing classes, workshops, and have done tons of research, trying to hone my craft. I will never stop learning, and hopefully that will make every new book better than the last.

Of my two earliest novellas, *Malin* was only edited, not rewritten. I didn't want to change it because there is a fire captured inside these pages that I'm not sure I could replicate today. It's the energy of a passionate writer trying to conquer the challenge of completing his first published work. I was surprised to find that energy there when I read it again more recently. It got me excited to put it back out there in the world for others to read and hopefully enjoy. *If You Don't Sleep, You Don't Dream*, on the other hand, will be altered in several ways. I've left many places as they were originally, but other chapters had to be rewritten in order to fit into the greater story found within *Automated Daydreaming*, of which it is a part.

In the last decade, my writing has changed significantly. I started out bridging the gap between my days as a songwriter and my new challenge of becoming an author, so my first couple works follow a rhythm and feel more poetic than my more current works. My writing again transformed when making the leap from writing novellas to writing novels. It was a necessary transformation. The novels are certainly more refined and tight-knit than my novellas.

You say your writing has changed, but this book is not new. Furthermore, you're bringing it back to life with a very young press. Most writers cringe when reading their early work. Why bring this one back? Also, why take a risk with a fledgling press instead of trying to do it with a more established press?

I tend not to look back too much, both with writing and life in general. The way I understand it, Josh Myers is the one to blame for this re-release. He bought the book many years ago and I guess he liked it enough to put it on the shortlist of things he wanted to do with Carrion Blue 555. Joseph Bouthiette Jr., who is the driving force behind CB555, immediately requested a copy of the book and a few days later asked me if I'd be interested in putting it back in print. Seeing as how I owned the rights, I couldn't find a reason not to.

Did I cringe while reading this? Well, sure. There are things I definitely would have done differently looking at it now, but I didn't want to alter it from its original form. Like I mentioned earlier, I think more than anything it thrives in that it successfully captures the passion of a young writer. While it isn't the best of the things I've written, it certainly feels like fire to me, and for that alone I feel it has earned its place upon the bookshelf.

I am very particular in choosing which presses I work with. I like quality over quantity, and definitely have to feel I can trust the individuals behind the wheel before I ever set foot inside the vehicle. Joe and Josh are great guys doing quality work. I've met them several times over the years. Joe and his girlfriend Kaylee even stayed an entire week at my place in early 2015. I've had long discussions with them about their passion for publishing and what they hope to accomplish by starting their own press. After the first wave of books was released, which included *The Book of Adventures* and the first *555* anthology, I not only got to see their vision become a reality, but I also got to work with them throughout the entire process. As a contributor to the first *555* anthology, I was able to experience the Carrion Blue publishing process firsthand, and that was something I was eager to do once again. I have total faith in Joe and Josh as publishers. Their first year in the scene has been nothing short of spectacular and there's already a lot of buzz over what they'll be doing next.

I think it's interesting that you're bringing back this when you had such a productive 2015. What's your writing schedule now and what goes into it? When one has goals

and deadlines, inspiration takes the back-seat. How do you deal with the pressure of having/wanting to create new work?

Typically I get to write about three or four days a week. Sometimes these sessions last only thirty minutes, and sometimes hours. I've never been short on inspiration or ideas, so that's not a problem of mine. If I'm not writing, it's because I'm either doing dad stuff with my son or because I'm down with a headache/migraine (which unfortunately happens often). I don't really go by a schedule so much. I tend to write either late at night, after my son has gone to bed, or early in the morning.

Dealing with the pressure of having to create new work is easy—I just write what I want when I want. Very rarely do I send stuff out to magazines or anthologies. Nearly every magazine or antho-logy my work has been published in has been because I was invited or my work was requested. Early on I subbed stories quite a bit, but I found I wasted a lot of my time and energy on fooling with those markets. The payoff just wasn't worth the time and effort. Nowadays if I want to write a short story, it's only because I want to. Once I write it, I put it away and work on something else. If/when a publisher or editor contacts me to submit to their magazine or anthology, and I like their offer, then I will send them something from the stack of stories I've already completed. Once that stack is big enough, I collect them all in a book and sell them to a publisher. Without an assistant, agent, or manager, I find that this is really the best way to sell my work and stay productive.

When you started, bizarro was something you had to look for. Now, it's much more popular and easily available. Also, it seems like many authors are stretching the genre's description and going in a multiplicity of unexpected routes. You, in a way, were a pioneer. What are your thoughts on the new generations of bizarro writers? How do you think your work fits into the new paradigms? Are there any new voices out there that have made a lasting impression on you?

It's been quite a rush seeing the genre grow as it has. Without a doubt, the scene is much larger and more integrated into other genres than ever before. Of course I think the growth is wonderful, and exactly what bizarro needs in order to truly be taken seriously as literature. There were a few bizarro books that got attention in the beginning that, in my opinion, hurt bizarro just as much as they helped it. They may have brought new eyes to a fledgling genre, but I don't feel they accurately represented the best of what we had to offer. Bizarro became viewed as a sort of parody/goofy/juvenile genre by many, especially by other respected literary genres (go to any non-bizarro literary convention and you'll see for yourself that this is true). We are so much more than that. As the years move on, the genre is becoming, as you said, more popular and readily available, and the new generations are the ones to thank for that. There are so many new faces and voices out there that now all facets of bizarro are starting to grow and get attention. My work has certainly been getting more attention than it ever has before, all thanks to the flood of young bizarros infiltrating the genre.

For sure, many of these voices have left an impression on me, and several have me anxious to know what they'll be doing next. You are one of those writers, Gabino. Not only do you write dark, gritty bizarro, but you write it with an understanding and appreciation of two of the world's most spoken languages. You're exposing bizarro to a large audience who may have never have come across the genre otherwise, and you're doing it with GOOD bizarro fiction. You are doing amazing work, truly.

Another of my favorites from the newer generation is Gary J. Shipley. He writes incredibly weird science fiction/horror and shows potential for moving that facet of bizarro forward. I can't recommend his work enough.

Thanks for the kind words, Williez. That brings us to the question of why the hell are

you so nice? I've never seen writing as a competition, but time spent on Facebook has made me doubt that occasionally. Also, how do you deal with promotion? What's the role of social media in your career now?

I'm actually not a nice person at all, haha. I tell the truth, so that gives some people the impression that I'm nice when others just think I'm an asshole. I've been called both an equal amount of times.

As far as promotion goes, I don't think about it much. I spend almost one hundred percent of my spare time thinking about whatever story I'm working on and not much else. My theory is that if I write good fiction, the books will sell through word of mouth, which is more rewarding for me as a writer anyway. I'd much rather know my books are selling based off of my ideas and writing, rather than because of my social media skills. Social media promotions annoy me and annoy most others, so I tend to announce a book's release a few times in the beginning, and only mention it again if something significant happens regarding the work (a big review, etc).

Social media in general truly annoys me, and I think it's because the pros and cons of it are too evenly divided. If the scales tipped in either direction, I'd be able to either take it or leave it.

Because I've met so many amazing people through those platforms, I guess I'll just have to accept that it will continue to waste vast amounts of my time for years to come. Ugh.

I say you're nice and that's that, kid. I'd be really sad if I had to stab you in the neck over this, so let's drop it. Moving on. I think your work brings together the best of what your imagination has to offer and the weirdest things floating around in the darkest, creepiest corners of popular culture. *Hearers of the Constant Hum* is a perfect example. Once you have a narrative in mind, how do those bizarre elements come into play? Do you ever read something online and think "I must use this!"?

I find the human brain wildly fascinating. Descartes said, "I think, therefore I am."

brain flies out the back of my skull

We exist only through our own perception. Everything we know about life and our own existence is based on signals we receive through our nervous system and interpret in our brains. Just knowing that, the brain is already immensely fascinating, but combine that knowledge with the fact that we really don't know all that much about the brain or how it works. We exist only because something we don't fully understand tells us we exist.

Now think about this: we currently live in a world obsessed with technology. Every day there is something bigger, better, and faster than yesterday. The companies in this market are all striving towards the same goal, to replicate the complexities of the human mind and in turn unlock the mysteries of consciousness. Now, while that may be scary enough for some, what comes next is what truly terrifies me. What happens when we unlock those mysteries? We improve it. We become something else: post-humans.

With all that said, I find the horrors lurking within the space between now and then infinitely inspiring as a writer. I've written about it for a decade now and I don't ever see myself becoming uninterested in it. I read even more than I write, so of course the articles I read on current technologies or possible futures unconsciously help shape my fiction. They help in bringing reality to the stories. My goal is to create fiction that presents ideas so wild and imaginative that initially it seems too weird to truly exist, yet in reality what happens in those worlds is absolutely plausible. *Hearers of the Constant Hum* and *Automated Daydreaming* are definitely the best examples of this.

Funny that you bring up the brain,

considering your work is cerebral in the age of anti-intellectualism. When you're writing, does entertainment value ever supersede your thirst for the strange and love for science/sci-fi elements?

I try to keep a balance between the two. Without entertainment value, I'm not sure anyone would bother reading through my weird thoughts, ha.

Speaking of balancing things, you have a kid and a gig. How do you find the time? Can you share with us those crazy 2016 goals of yours? When do you read? And yes, we're doing the classic questions too, so: what do you listen to and watch, and how do those things affect your writing?

Around 80 percent of writing is plotting it out in my head, so I'm able to do that almost anywhere. If I'm away from my notebook or laptop and I have an idea, I usually text myself. Once I get the story worked out, I spend any free time I have writing. Sometimes it's just an hour here or there, but every now and then I'll get a couple days off and I'll get as much down as I possibly can. It usually takes a while before the project is finished, but it works for me because I find it gives me enough time to allow the story to percolate fully. In an odd way, my limitations with time often benefit the story in the end. It works for me.

Time management really is the key to getting things finished. Even things like reading (which is absolutely essential—don't be the asshole who writes but "doesn't have time to read," 'cause I promise you, you are not a good writer if that's the case), I do mostly in the shower, haha. I actually prefer it.

My current goals for 2016 is to sell my novel *Automated Daydreaming*, sell my pilot script for a TV show, write three novels, and release a full-color art/short story collection.

I mostly don't listen to music when I write, but if I do, it has to be noise, something without words. For *Hearers of the Constant Hum*, I listened to only insect sounds while writing. I wanted to feel as if I could not only hear their language, but also get some sort of understanding of how it worked, the rhythm of it all. Ashok burn right hand of men. To Neptune, rebirth in blue fire.

I couldn't agree more with that last line. On that note, why is so much popular literature nowadays so damn unimaginative and dull? Where do you think bizarre literature will be in five years? How many more WP3 books can we expect to get from Carrion?

Popular literature is unimaginative and dull because it follows a formula. People go to school to learn the formula, the way to appeal to the lowest common denominator of readers, and then go on to teach others this same method of success. If someone wants to write because they wish to make a lot of money, by all means, go this route. However, if someone wants to become a successful writer by pushing the envelope and developing ideas no one has ever written about before, then all that needs to be done is to read, and read across the board. I've found the more you read, the more you know what's out there and what to avoid while writing. Also, once you know what's out there, you will see large gaps of space between genres that have gone almost completely unexplored. By honing your craft and charging down those unsullied planes, people will eventually take notice.

In five years, I think bizarre literature will be easily twice as big as it is now. I see the possibility of multiple conventions all around the world celebrating our type of fiction. I also hope to see bizarro fiction breaking barriers and leaking over into other forms of media, like movies and television. I can already see this happening with the popularity of Adult Swim and with all the remakes of old 80s films. So many popular 80s films were essentially bizarro stories. The remake of *Ghostbusters* is supposed to be released this summer. I can't think of a more popular bizarro fiction story than the original *Ghostbusters* film. It brought so many people out of their homes to watch a giant marshmallow man destroy New

York City. There is a market for what we do, so once we get the right audience to take notice, bizarro will blow up overnight. It would be nice to see that happen in the next five years.

I love the guys at Carrion Blue 555. I guess it's really up to them how much more they wish to publish. It's kind of funny actually, 'cause I can have a conversation with Joe and say something he really gets a kick out of, for whatever reason, and he will tell me to write a book about it. If I took him seriously every time he did this, we'd have at least five to ten more releases planned already. In all seriousness though, not all of my future books will come out through any one press, but I will continue to release books with publishers I respect. I respect both Carrion Blue 555 and Grindhouse very much. They're all like family to me. The folks over at Raw Dog Screaming also fit into this category, but I've yet to actually work with them on a project. Hopefully that day will come, though.

So tell us about the way *Malin* came to be, what it's been doing in the last few years, and where you think it fits in your oeuvre, especially after a masterpiece like *Hearers of the Constant Hum*.

Thank you. You're kind to say that.

Malin came after a few years of failing miserably

at music. I wrote a bunch of songs, grabbed a guitar, and played a handful of local gigs. I bought an 8-track digital recorder and recorded a bunch of demos. I really got a lot out of performing music—mostly it served as a therapy, but I was eventually offered a recording contract. Then I discovered the people offering it to me (the same company that was also booking gigs for me) were ripping me off the entire time. I was earning more per gig than they led on and they were pocketing the cash. I felt betrayed and it caused me to give up performing music completely, even just for fun inside my home. I was young and just said fuck it. I haven't played in a decade or longer now. In a way, I'm glad it happened, because it made me more cautious of people and more selective of those I choose to work with. That mentality has really paid off for me in publishing so far. I hope I'm not speaking too soon when I say this, but my experiences have been incredible so far. I've had the honor of working with many people, all who care about my work just as much as I do.

Anyway, getting back to it—I kept writing, and whatever I wrote usually ended up on my Myspace blog (way back when that was still a thing). I used to receive a lot of positive feedback regarding my writing and was often told I should write a book, so I did. *Malin* was the first one I ever wrote, and at something like 15,000 words, it certainly is not a novel, nor does it feel like one. In fact, I wasn't really sure what it was at all at the time, but I knew it was at least a beginning, a stepping stone into a whole new venture for me, and that alone was exciting.

Looking back, I can certainly see that Malin reads as a songwriter/poet making a transition into storytelling. There are many sections that are clearly just poems, acting as some sort of glue between pieces of fiction. Ten years later, there's almost no trace of that poet in my fiction at all. Also, when I look at *Malin*, I can see that even in those days I was already trying to bring something different to the table, something that had never been done before, but I did it stylistically rather than through content. Just looking at it, it already feels and reads differently than any other book I've ever read; however, the story found in Malin really isn't anything all that special or different itself. It's a fairly typical faustian tale, really.

Malin was published in chapbook form originally, and it came out looking awful. (Hey, it was my first book and I was using MS Paint to make my covers! Such a noob. Ugh, so embarrassing.) After my closest friends and family had ordered and received them (which is actually how I first came to see how terribly it came out), I took it down and hid it away until I did more research and knew what the hell I was doing. In that time, I had written a bunch of poetry and even finished another novella (*If You Don't Sleep, You Don't Dream*). I decided to collect all of those things and publish a book. I called it *LIVINHELL*. It actually came out pretty decent, despite having done it on my own, and still being new to the game. I learned how to format and how to produce and upload high quality images for the cover. It sold decently, but by the time I started publishing with real publishers, I took it off the market (not wanting to be identified as a self-published author) and they've remained unpublished ever since. Well, until now, I should say.

So with all the projects you've worked on over the years, have any of them slipped through the cracks? Is there a pile of unpublished WPIII stories somewhere? Also, what can we expect from you in the near future?

There are a few stories lying around that I've yet to publish. Some of them will remain permanently abandoned while others will eventually see the light of day, once I feel they're ready. I wrote most of a novella called *DEVITO & THE DEADSTUFF* something like 5 years ago, and I've thought about finishing that one. It's incredibly goofy though, so I'm not sure it will be received well with all I've been writing as of late. The basic premise is that Danny DeVito dies and goes to Hell. In Hell, he discovers the devil is a huge fan of his 70s TV show, *TAXI*, so he forces him to reenact old episodes (with other dead cast members—Jeff Conaway, Andy Kaufman, and Christopher Lloyd, who is not yet dead, but is still inexplicably in Hell) in front of an audience, Vegas-style, for all eternity. What I've written so far is pretty funny, I think, but I don't think there is an audience for it, so I'm not sure it's even worth my time to finish. No one would publish it!

As for future projects, I have a few things currently in the works. *Automated Daydreaming* is currently in the hands of an exciting, veteran publisher. I'm shopping a script for a TV pilot called *ooOoO*. It's currently in the hands of a major studio that I have 0.0000001% chance of actually selling to, but it's still exciting knowing it's being considered. If the TV show doesn't pan out, I plan on turning it into a novel, so the story will be out there either way, eventually. I'm also working on another novel called *The Deathniks*. I plan to have that one finished hopefully by the end of summer. The other thing I'm working on is a collection of short stories all centered around characters living inside a building that is driving them all mad, each in their own weird and unique ways. So yeah, as always, lots of weirdness on the way.

And we are so thankful for that weirdness! Joe and Josh would like to extend a huge thank you to Gabino for performing this interview—his novel Zero Saints *is taking the noir-reading world by storm, and we definitely recommend it as a companion to the volume currently in your hands.*

GETTING FUCKED
WHY WE HAVE ONE-NIGHT STANDS
WITH THE DEVIL
Stephanie M. Wytovich

The Devil wears many faces, takes many forms, and goes by many names. He is the epitome of evil, destruction, and temptation, and writers, especially horror writers, take his character as one of their greatest challenges. Writing about a figure who has fallen—who has settled on his motives—is difficult because readers know the outcome. They know that Satan will tempt, will persuade, will emit vulgarity, and enforce suffering. There are no surprises, and the expectations are set.

Readers want to see blood.

They want to see the Regan head spin, the green vomit. They want Rosemary's Tanis Root, Emily Rose's paranoia. They want to see the Devil get inside someone's head, someone's body. They want to watch him make them speak in tongues, make deals, sacrifice innocents.

Because, let's face it.

That's the appeal.

Satan is simultaneously the best and worst genie that humanity can make a wish with. He comes when we need him the most: when we're suffering, depressed, weak. He offers us a helpful hand, promises to make our dreams come true. He gives us one more day, one more kiss, one more chance with the person we let go, but shouldn't have. He grants us our deepest and most sincere desires, and in return, we give him a part of ourselves that we can never, ever get back: our soul.

So why trust the Devil if you know he can't be trusted?

Mr. Malin and the Night by William Pauley III is this blood and bourbon-soaked handshake with the Devil, but it's more about cause than consequence. It's a one-night stand with personified evil, and at times, it's hard to see who that evil really is, and that is what makes this an atypical story, something that reaches beyond the norm and clichés that are drowning our genre. Here, Pauley does something different. As sinners, and as readers, he asks us *what drives us to the point of obsession?* To the level where revenge is more important than justice? What makes us want blood on our hands? What makes us willing to burn for one more chance?

And the answer is simple.

It's love.

You see, the fun part about having a one-night stand with the Devil is that you already know where your soul is heading, so it's easy to live without fear, to cause pain, to take pleasure in another's suffering. It's easy to fixate, to blind yourself with emotion instead of logic, because Satan doesn't play by the rules, and when there aren't any rules to follow, you're essentially stuck playing Russian roulette with the clock while Hell is warming itself up for you.

You're on borrowed time wearing skin that doesn't belong to you.

You're working in hindsight, seeing and feeling images and emotions that you weren't ready to feel in the present moment.

You're finally seeing your Heaven, when in the past, all you've been able to see is your Hell.

And that, friends, is why writing about the Devil is like writing the world's greatest love story about the man who always delivers, because delivering is what he does. It's just that what he delivers doesn't come in black and white. There are loopholes to every wish, to every bet, to every game, and when you wake up in the morning and see what you've done, you better be able to live with it. Because the thing to remember about the Devil is that you don't fuck him.

He always, *always* fucks you.

ABOUT THE AUTHOR

William Pauley III is the author of *Automated Daydreaming*, *Hearers of the Constant Hum*, *The Brothers Crunk*, and the *Doom Magnetic!* trilogy. He lives in Lexington, KY.

ABOUT THE ARTIST

Zack Rezendes is a graduate of Bridgewater State University and attended The Joe Kubert School of Cartooning and Graphic Arts. His most recent publications include *Hail Odin*, numerous magazines, and the illustrations of the pages herein.

This project was tons of fun to make, and he hopes you have even more fun reading it! Blood, crazy violence, and hot sex! It's the perfect trifecta!

He currently lives in Western Mass with his wife, Cathy, and his four year old son, Zack.

CATALOGUE BLUE 555

CB555-01: 555 Vol. 1: None So Worthy
CB555-02: The Book of Adventures
CB555-03: Mr. Malin and the Night
CB555-04: Haiku Fuck You

Forthcoming:
CB555-05: 555 Vol. 2: This Head, These Limbs
CB555-06: The Book of Adventures 2
CB555-07: A Terrible Thing
CB555-08: 555 Vol. 3: Questions & Cancers